Stark County District Library
Jackson Township Branch
7487 Fulton Drive NW
Massillon, OH 44646
330.833.1010
www.starklibrary.org

DISCARD

# Getting into Hockey

**Ron Thomas and Joe Herran**

A Haights Cross Communications Company®
Philadelphia

This edition first published in 2006 in the United States of America by Chelsea House Publishers,
a subsidiary of Haights Cross Communications.

A Haights Cross Communications Company®

All rights reserved. No part of this publication may be reproduced or transmitted in any form or
by any means without the written permission of the publisher.

Chelsea House Publishers
2080 Cabot Boulevard West, Suite 201
Langhorne, PA 19047-1813

The Chelsea House world wide web address is www.chelseahouse.com

First published in 2005 by
MACMILLAN EDUCATION AUSTRALIA PTY LTD
627 Chapel Street, South Yarra 3141

Visit our website at www.macmillan.com.au

Associated companies and representatives throughout the world.

Copyright © Ron Thomas and Joe Herran 2005

Library of Congress Cataloguing-in-Publication Data Applied for.
ISBN 0 7910 8810 3

Edited by Helena Newton
Text and cover design by Cristina Neri, Canary Graphic Design
Illustrations by Nives Porcellato and Andy Craig
Photo research by Legend Images

Printed in China

**Acknowledgments**
The authors wish to acknowledge and thank Keith Needham for his assistance and advice in the
writing of this book.

The authors and the publisher are grateful to the following for permission to reproduce copyright
material:

Cover photographs: Hockey ball courtesy of Photolibrary.com, and player courtesy of Picture Media/
REUTERS/Eliana Aponte.

Australian Picture Library, pp. 5, 7 (left); Shaun Botterill/Allsport/Getty Images, p. 24; Timothy A.
Clary/AFP/Getty Images, p. 23; Indranil Mukherjee/AFP/Getty Images, p. 9; Aamir Qureshi/AFP/Getty
Images, pp. 7 (right), 22; Photolibrary.com, pp. 1, 6, 26, 27; Picture Media/ REUTERS/Eliana Aponte, p.
30; Picture Media/REUTERS/Bazuki Muhammad, p. 28; Picture Media/REUTERS/Kai Pfaffenbach, p. 20;
Picture Media/REUTERS/Jason Reed, p. 4; Picture Media/REUTERS/Max Thomas, p. 29.

While every care has been taken to trace and acknowledge copyright, the publisher tenders their
apologies for any accidental infringement where copyright has proved untraceable. Where the attempt
has been unsuccessful, the publisher welcomes information that would redress the situation.

# Contents

The game  4

Equipment  6

Clothing  7

The pitch  8

The players  9

Skills  10

Rules  22

Scoring and timing  23

Umpires  24

Player fitness  26

Competition  28

Olympic hockey  30

Glossary  31

Index  32

**Glossary words**

When a word is printed in **bold**, you can look up its meaning in the Glossary on page 31.

# The game

Hockey is a popular sport with both young and older people who play in local, district, and state teams. There is also an indoor version of hockey.

Hockey is a team game played mainly in winter in many countries around the world. Hockey competition is governed by the International Hockey Federation (FIH), which was founded in Paris in 1924. The FIH is responsible for international hockey rules and competitions, and for promoting hockey internationally.

## History of hockey

Hockey may have begun many centuries ago in Egypt. A tomb painting dating from about 2050 B.C. shows two players with curved sticks and a ball. The ancient Greeks and Romans played a game similar to hockey, as did the Aztec people of ancient Mexico. In England, a hockey-like game called bandy ball was played until 1365 when it was banned by King Edward III because it was too rough and dangerous. The first hockey rules were drawn up in the 1860s in England and the modern game spread from there.

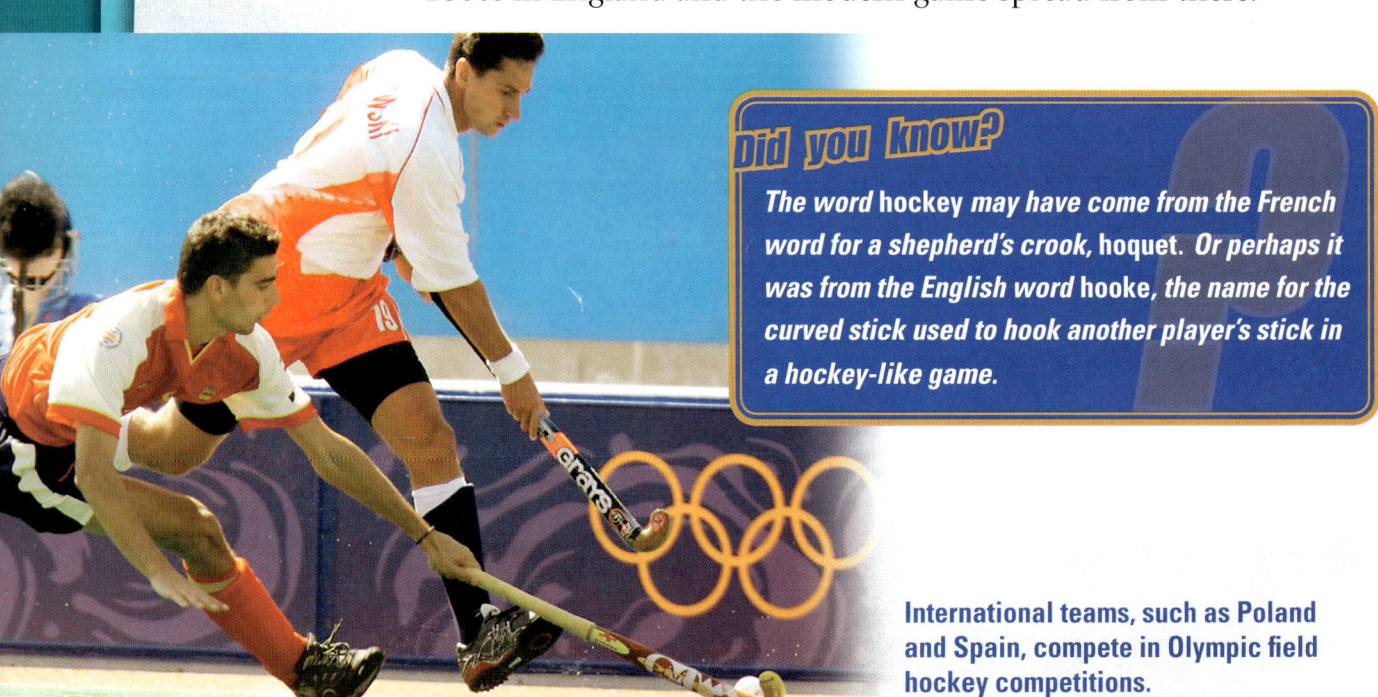

### Did you know?

*The word* hockey *may have come from the French word for a shepherd's crook,* hoquet. *Or perhaps it was from the English word* hooke, *the name for the curved stick used to hook another player's stick in a hockey-like game.*

**International teams, such as Poland and Spain, compete in Olympic field hockey competitions.**

## Playing a match

Two teams of 11 players compete against each other in a hockey match. Both teams aim to score more goals than the opposing team. Using their hooked sticks, 10 field players on each side try to gain control of the small, hard ball and then hit, **push**, **pass**, and **dribble** it along the field and into the goal. The 11$^{th}$ player of each team, the goalkeeper, tries to stop the opposing team from scoring by keeping the ball out of the goal. Only the goalkeepers are allowed to use their hands, feet, or other parts of their bodies to stop or move the ball.

**Hockey players aim to get control of the ball using long, hooked sticks.**

Two umpires, one in each half of the **pitch**, control the game. The game starts with a **pass-back** from the center of the field. A pass-back is also used to begin the second half of the game and after a goal has been scored. A hockey match is played in two halves of 35 minutes each. The team with the most goals at the end of 70 minutes is the winner. If the match ends in a tie, extra time is played and the first team to score in the extra time wins.

# Equipment

The equipment used for hockey is the same for men and women. Players select a stick of a length and weight that suits their height and build. Specially designed sticks and balls are available for junior players.

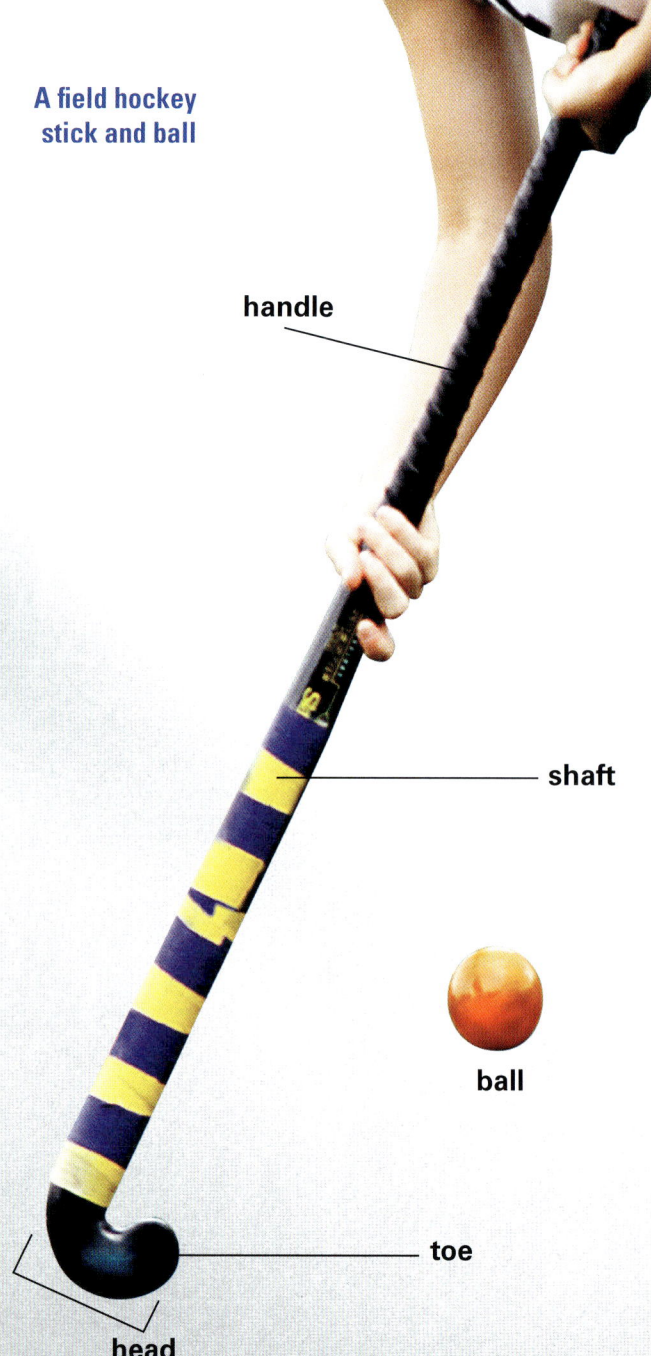

A field hockey stick and ball

handle

shaft

ball

toe

head

## Stick

The field hockey stick is made of wood, fiberglass, or **kevlar** and is about 3 feet (1 meter) long. It can weigh up to 28 ounces (794 grams). The stick has a curved head that is flat on one side and rounded on the other. Only the flat side of the stick, called the blade, and the edges can be used to strike the ball. The section of the stick between the handle and head is called the shaft and the curved end of the stick is called the toe.

## Ball

A hockey ball is round and usually white but can also be orange. It is made of cork or plastic and has a hard, usually smooth, outer covering of plastic to keep it waterproof. Some hockey balls are dimpled like golf balls.

# Clothing

Hockey clothing is comfortable and allows for easy movement. Men wear shorts and short-sleeved shirts. Women players usually wear skirts and shirts.

## Boots and socks

Boots need to fit well and support the feet. When playing on grass, nylon or rubber studs are placed in the soles of the boots for a better grip. Socks absorb sweat and keep the feet comfortable. Socks also keep the shin guards in place.

## Protective clothing

Shin guards made of plastic with foam inner linings are worn inside the socks to protect the shins. Mouthguards that protect the teeth are recommended for all players.

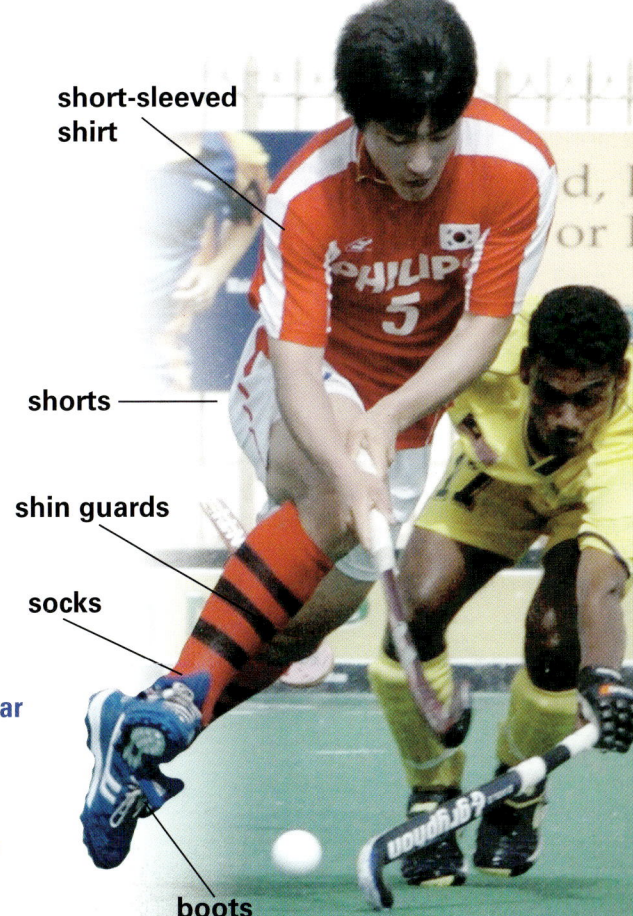

- short-sleeved shirt
- shorts
- shin guards
- socks
- boots

- helmet
- shoulder pads
- chest pad
- gloves
- padded shorts
- leg guards
- "kickers" covering the front and sides of the shoes

**Goalkeepers wear different colors from the rest of the team and must wear extra protective gear.**

### Rules

*Protective headgear is compulsory for goalkeepers, except when they take a penalty stroke.*

*Captains must wear an identifying armband or a special piece of cloth on their shoulder.*

# The pitch

Field hockey is played on a rectangular-shaped area called the pitch. Hockey is traditionally played on grass, but is now often played on synthetic or artificial surfaces. The pitch is 180 feet (55 meters) wide and 300 feet (91.4 meters) long. Flagposts are placed at each corner of the pitch. Each team aims to get the ball into the goal at the opposite end of the pitch from where they begin play.

**A hockey pitch**

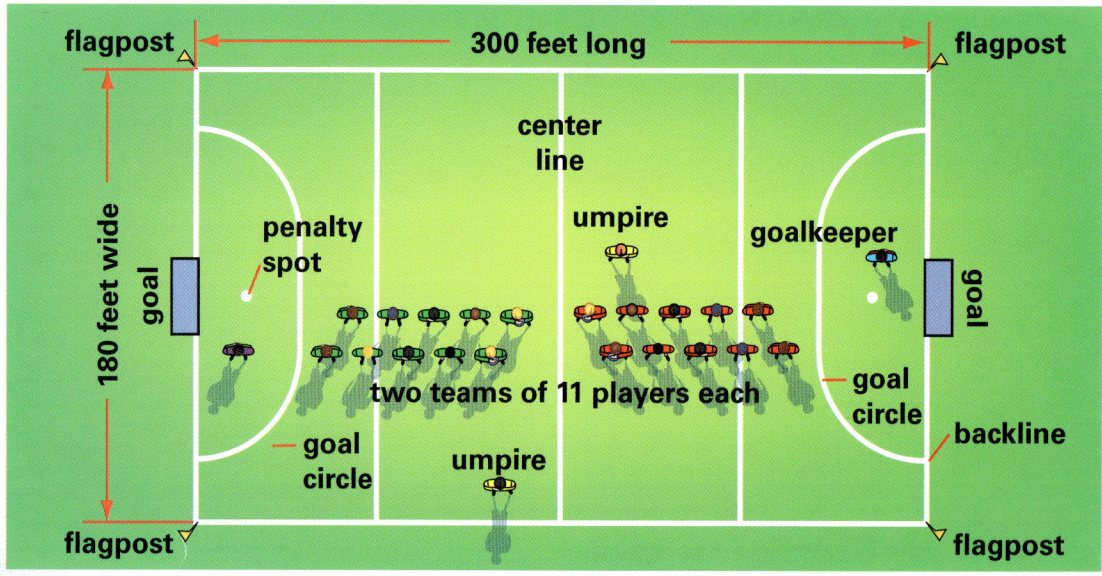

**A hockey goal**

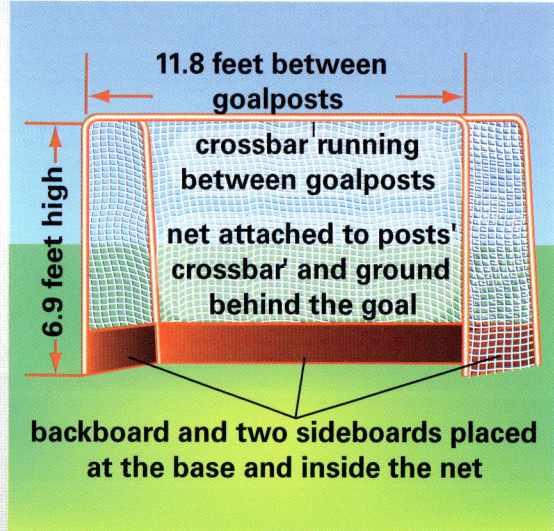

## Goals and goal circle

The goals are at the center of the backlines. Goals consist of two goalposts, a **crossbar**, and a net. The goal circle is actually a D-shaped area made up of two quarter-circles out from each goalpost and joined by a short straight line. It is also known as the "shooting circle" or "striking circle."

**Rule**

*A player must be within the goal circle to score a goal.*

# The players

All players except the goalkeeper are called field players. During a game, players are either:

- **attackers**, in possession of the ball and moving it forward to try to score a goal
- **defenders**, positioned near the goalkeeper, trying to stop the opposition from scoring a goal and trying to take the ball from their opponents
- **midfielders**, doing a bit of both.

Attacking hockey players adopt a well-balanced attack stance. They stand behind the ball with the stick on the ground.

Defending hockey players, whose job is to take the ball away from an opponent, adopt a well-balanced stance with one foot forward. The weight is on the balls of the feet and the player is ready to change directions quickly.

Defending hockey players aim to take the ball away from the attacking player.

## Player positions at the start of the game

At the start of the game, all players must be in their own half of the field and the defending team must be at least 16.5 feet (5 meters) from the ball.

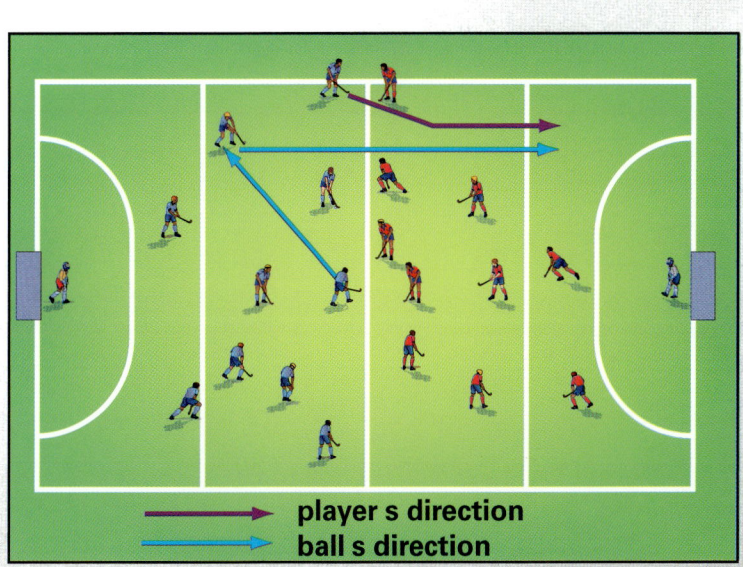

The game begins with a pass-back.

player's direction
ball's direction

# Skills

Beginning players learn the basic skills of hockey, which include handling the stick, dribbling, receiving the ball, passing the ball to teammates, and shooting for goal. They also learn to **tackle** an opponent to gain possession of the ball. Goalkeepers must learn to stop shots from going into the goal. With practice, players will develop these skills and improve their performance.

**In the correct hockey grip, the player forms V shapes with both thumbs and forefingers.**

## The grip

To be able to control, pass, push, stop, and shoot the ball well, the player must grip the stick correctly. The player holds the stick with the left hand at the top and the right hand about 12 inches (30 centimeters), or halfway down, the handle. Both thumbs and forefingers form V shapes.

## Turning the stick

All players play right-handed. To play left-side shots, the player reverses the stick by loosening the grip of the right hand and turning the stick counterclockwise with the left hand.

**To play a shot to the left, the stick is reversed so that the ball is struck with the blade.**

### Did you know?

There are no left-handed hockey sticks. All sticks are the same and are used by players who are right- or left-handed.

10

## Running with and without the ball

Hockey players must run with and without the ball. They need to be able to run backward, sideways, and forward at a jogging speed and at a sprint. The player runs with the ball in an open space when there are no opponents close by. The stick and the ball are well out in front of the body and slightly to the right as the player runs at speed. The player **scans** ahead, looking for opponents and planning the next move.

**The player holds the stick out in front of the body when running with the ball.**

## Running with the stick

Hockey players must be able to run swiftly with the stick, keeping their balance at all times. When the player is near the ball, both hands grip the stick, ready to receive a pass. Players who are farther away from the ball and moving into position can grip the stick with only the right hand and pump their arms as they run for greater speed.

**The player who is not near the ball grips the stick in the right hand only while running.**

*SKILLS*

**SKILLS**

## Stop and turn

An attacking player running forward to receive a pass uses a stop and turn to change directions. With the stick held in both hands, the player runs forward quickly. To stop, the player plants one foot firmly on the ground, pivots on the balls of the feet, and pushes off in a new direction.

**The stop and turn**

## Dribbling

Dribbling is also running with the ball, but the player keeps the ball close and under control using short taps of the stick.

Dribbling is used to:
- move the ball down the pitch
- outmaneuver opponents
- keep possession of the ball.

**Rules**
*The stick must be smooth and not have any rough or sharp parts.*

*Players must not lift their sticks over the heads of other players.*

**The player dribbling the ball must show skill in controlling both the stick and the ball.**

When dribbling, the player:
- keeps the ball in front and on the right side of the body, away from the feet
- bends the knees and stays low over the ball
- watches the ball and looks where he or she is going
- scans and is always prepared to change speed, direction, and tactic.

## Indian dribble

To perform the Indian dribble, the player moves the ball along from side to side, using a rolling wrist action to tap or drag the ball from left to right in front of the body.

**The Indian dribble**

**Did you know?**

The best hockey players in the world can dribble without looking at the ball. This is called using "touch control."

## Dodging

Dodging is used to dribble past an opponent. The player moves in one direction to make an opponent think that the player is about to move in that direction. As the opponent tries to block the move, the player quickly changes direction and passes the opponent.

## Receiving the ball

Receiving the ball means trapping it with the stick, and then controlling and moving it into position for a dribble, pass, or shot at goal. The player receiving the ball:

- notices how fast the ball is moving
- chooses the best position to receive the pass
- scans for opponents
- decides what will be done with the ball once it is trapped.

### Forehand receiving

To receive the ball forehand, the player's left shoulder points toward the oncoming ball. The stick is held upright and the player moves toward the ball. With the stick head close to the ground, the player allows the ball to come onto the stick, near the right foot. The face of the stick is tilted toward the ground to stop the ball rebounding upward. The player is now ready to pass, shoot, or dribble.

**Receiving the ball forehand must be done quickly to prevent opponents from taking it.**

## Reverse or backhand receiving

For reverse or backhand receiving, the player's right shoulder points toward the oncoming ball and the stick is held in the **reverse stick** position, so that the toe of the stick faces the player's feet. The ball is received close to the left foot with the stick face angled toward the ground. This traps the ball and stops it from rebounding. The stick is then reversed and the player is ready to pass, dribble, or shoot for goal.

**When receiving the ball on the reverse side of the stick, the player relaxes the right-hand grip to stop the ball from bouncing away.**

**The ball can also be received with the stick angled to the ground.**

## Receiving an aerial ball

To receive an aerial ball, the player, holding the stick below shoulder height, moves into line with the ball. The face of the stick is angled downward so that the ball will land close to the right foot. The knees are bent as the ball hits the stick below the right hand and in front of the body. The ball is brought under control and the player moves on.

**For an aerial trap, the ball must be below shoulder height when it is played on the stick.**

15

## Passing the ball

A pass involves two players: the passer and the receiver. In order to make a good pass, the player must decide:

- when to pass
- in which direction to pass
- how fast to pass
- what sort of shot to play.

### Forehand push pass

The forehand push pass is the most common way of passing the ball. To perform the forehand push pass, the player follows these steps.

**The forehand push pass**

1 The player is sideways, with the left foot and shoulder facing in the direction the ball is to travel. The stick is next to the ball and angled toward the ground to stop the ball from bouncing upward.

2 The ball is pushed with the head of the stick.

3 The player follows through with the stick, in line with the target.

## Flick

The **flick** is a push pass that lifts the ball into the air. It is used to pass the ball over an opponent. The ball in front of the player's left foot and the stick head is placed under the ball. The crouching player flicks the ball upward and forward.

**The flick**

# Hitting the ball

Players hit the ball to drive it quickly over long distances, for free hits, and for shots at goal. The player follows these steps to hit the ball.

**The hit**

1 The player grips the stick with both hands close together, and steps in with the left shoulder and leg pointing toward the target. The stick is behind the right shoulder.

2 The stick is swung through to hit the ball.

3 The player follows through with the stick in the direction of the ball.

## Shooting for goal

Scoring more goals than the opposition is the aim of hockey. To score goals, the player must learn to hit, flick, push, chip, and redirect the ball in the direction of the goal. There are several types of goal shots.

### Quick hit

The quick hit is also called the "short-grip." The player's left shoulder faces the goal and the front foot is in line with the ball. The knees are flexed for balance. Gripping the stick halfway down, the player uses a short, quick backswing before hitting the ball.

A quick hit is a fast shot at goal.

### Dive shot

The dive shot is also called the "slide shot." For this shot, the player sprints and dives to fully extend the stick toward the ball. The player slides along the ground on one side of the body with arms outstretched. The lower half of the ball is hit with the stick angled upward. The ball is lifted up and into the goal.

A dive or slide shot

18

### Edge shot

The edge shot is used for a ball that is rolling away from the shooter. Following a short backswing, the player moves into a crouched position and strikes the ball with the edge of the stick, with the flat side facing the sky. The hands are close together and close to the ground.

*The edge shot is also known as the tomahawk.*

### Chip shot

For a chip shot, the player slides the hands together and hits the lower half of the ball, sending it up in the air and toward the goal. The chip shot is similar to the hit.

**Rule**
*The edge shot and the chip shot are played only at senior levels.*

*A chip shot is used to beat a low-sliding goalkeeper.*

## Tackling

Tackling is used to try to take the ball away from an opponent. Timing the tackle and using the best tackle for the situation are important choices the player must make.

**The jab or poke tackle**

### Jab or poke tackle

To perform the jab or poke tackle, the player holds the stick in one hand. The player then makes a sudden **jab** at the ball.

**The block tackle**

### Block tackle

During the block tackle, the player forces the opponent to run onto the open face of the stick, to the right. The player then lays the stick flat on the ground to stop the shot.

**Rule**

A **penalty** is given against any player who interferes with or hits an opponent's stick when tackling.

### Reverse tackle

This is a difficult and dangerous tackle. The player moves close to the opponent without touching them and stays side-on, keeping the body low and the stick flat.

The reverse tackle requires a lot of practice.

## Goalkeeping

The goalkeeper's main job is to stop shots from going into the goal. When the ball is in the goal circle, the goalkeeper can play the ball with the stick, feet, hands, or protective clothing.

A good goalkeeper:
- has good balance
- has good reflexes
- has good footwork
- is able to guess what might happen next
- keeps the head and body in line with the path of the ball
- keeps the eyes focused on the ball.

> **Rules**
> The goalkeeper may use the stick, protective clothing, and any part of the body to stop or redirect the ball.
> The goalkeeper may raise the stick above shoulder height when making a save.

The goalkeeper moves toward the attacker to reduce the area available for the attacker to aim at. To save shots that are along or near the ground, the goalkeeper uses the stick, pads, or kickers to clear the ball. Whenever possible, the goalkeeper uses the pads and kickers to clear the ball and save a shot.

**A** Using a foot, the goalkeeper kicks the ball clear.
**B** A high shot at goal is saved using a gloved hand.
**C** Diving saves can be made to either side.

# Rules

Hockey rules for all international competitions are formulated by hockey's governing body, the International Hockey Federation (FIH). Players need to learn and understand the basic rules before they are ready to play hockey.

Here are some hockey rules from the FIH rule book:

- Players must not play the ball in a dangerous way. Hitting the ball so that it rises into the air can be called dangerous play.
- Field players must not stop, kick, pick up, throw, or carry the ball with any part of their body.
- Players must not tackle unless they are in a position to play the ball without coming into contact with an opponent.
- Goalkeepers must not take part in the match outside the half of the field they are defending, unless they are taking a penalty shot.

**Goalkeepers must stay close to the goal and within the half of the field they are defending.**

# Scoring and timing

Hockey goals are scored from the field, penalty corners, and penalty strokes. All goals are worth one point. A match is played in two 35-minute halves. The team with the most goals after 70 minutes wins. If the match is tied, the first team to score in extra time wins.

## Goals scored from the field

A goal is scored from the field by an attacker within the goal circle. The ball must pass over the goal line and under the crossbar.

## Penalty corners

The attacking team is awarded a penalty corner when:
- a defender intentionally sends the ball over the backline
- a defender **fouls** an opponent within the goal circle.

**Players in position for a penalty corner**

No more than five defenders and the goalie stand on the goal line. One attacker stands on the backline and pushes the ball to the attackers waiting in the goal circle. The defenders and goalkeeper cannot move until the ball is in play.

## Penalty strokes

A penalty stroke is awarded when a defender fouls an opponent in the goal circle, stopping a goal from being scored, or when a defender deliberately fouls an opponent who has the ball in the goal circle.

One player, chosen by the attacking team, shoots for goal from the penalty spot. Only the goalkeeper defends the goal.

# Umpires

Two umpires control a match, one in each half of the pitch. Umpires must know the rules and apply them fairly. Umpires:

- keep a record of goals scored
- keep a record of warnings to players and cards shown
- act as timekeepers.

Umpires award penalties against any player who:

- uses the stick or plays the ball dangerously
- touches or handles another player in a way that interferes with their game
- plays the ball with any part of the stick above shoulder height (except to stop a shot at goal)
- stops, picks up, throws, kicks, or carries the ball
- obstructs an opponent who is trying to play the ball
- wastes time.

## Cards

Umpires use cards to warn players about breaking rules. If a player deliberately breaks a rule, the umpire shows him or her a green card. A yellow card is shown to a player who uses rough play to deliberately foul another player. A player shown a yellow card is suspended from play and cannot rejoin the game for five minutes or longer. A red card is for a serious offense such as deliberately running into another player or verbally abusing officials. A player shown a red card must leave the field and cannot take any further part in the game.

*An umpire uses a card to caution a player.*

## Umpires' signals

Umpires use a whistle and hand signals to let players and other umpires and officials know of their decisions.

**These are some of the signals used by hockey umpires.**

One arm raised signals game time has started.

Arms crossed above head signals game time has stopped.

Both arms pointed horizontally toward corner of field signals a goal has been scored.

One arm raised horizontally with hand open at face level signals a free hit.

Pointing both arms horizontally toward the goal signals a penalty corner.

One arm pointing to the penalty area and the other raised overhead signals a penalty stroke.

Facing palms held horizontally and close together in front of the body signals a raised ball.

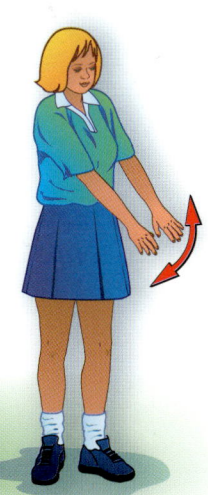
Moving both hands up and down in front of the body with palms down signals dangerous play or bad temper.

# Player fitness

Hockey players need to be fit if they are to perform to the best of their ability. Running, swimming, and cycling build stamina and fitness.

## Warming up and stretching

Before a game or a practice session, it is important for hockey players to warm up all their muscles. This helps prevent injuries such as muscle tears, strains, and joint injuries. Gentle jogging helps players warm up. Stretching makes players more flexible and helps the muscles and joints move easily.

### Neck stretches

The player tilts the head forward and slowly rolls the head to one shoulder and then the other. These exercises help prevent stiffness in the neck and keep the neck flexible.

### Side stretches

The player raises the right hand above the head and slowly leans to the left. Then the stretch is repeated, raising the left hand above the head and leaning slowly to the right.

### Hamstring stretch

The player sits on the ground with one leg extended in front of the body and the other knee bent. Bending forward slowly, the player reaches toward the toes.

**Performing hamstring stretches before playing hockey can help prevent hamstring injuries.**

### Calf stretches

The player places one foot in front of the other and leans forward, but keeps the back heel on the ground. The player pushes forward until the calf muscle in the back leg stretches. The stretch is repeated for the other leg.

**Stretching exercises, such as calf stretches, are done in an easy and relaxed way and each position is held for at least 10 seconds.**

### Thigh stretches

Standing on one leg, the player holds the ankle of the raised leg and pulls the foot back to stretch the thigh, keeping the knees close together. The player can lean against a goalpost or hold onto another player for balance. The stretch is repeated for the other leg.

### Back stretch

The player crouches down on all fours with the head up and back flat. Then the player tucks the head under and arches the back upward. The player feels the stretch in the upper back.

### Groin stretch

The player sits on the ground with the knees bent and pointing out to either side. Holding onto the ankles, the player pulls them gently in toward the body. The player pushes down gently on the thighs with the arms so that the legs move toward the ground.

# Competition

The world governing body for hockey is the International Hockey Federation (FIH). It is made up of 112 national associations from around the world and a network of five continental federations. The FIH's head office is in Brussels, Belgium. The FIH is responsible for:

- the rules of hockey
- all umpiring and coaching matters
- the organization of international tournaments
- the global development and promotion of the sport.

The German team won the Men's Hockey World Cup, held in Kuala Lumpur, Malaysia, in 2002.

## FIH international competitions

The FIH organizes the Men's Hockey World Cup, Men's Champions Trophy, and the European Hockey Cup.

### Men's World Cup

The first men's World Cup was held in Barcelona, Spain, in 1971 and is now held every four years. Teams in different parts of the world must win a series of qualifying games to advance to the finals of the World Cup. Past World Cup winners were:

- Pakistan, 1971
- Netherlands, 1973
- India, 1975
- Pakistan, 1978
- Pakistan, 1982
- Australia, 1986
- Netherlands, 1990
- Pakistan, 1994
- Netherlands, 1998
- Germany, 2002.

### Men's Champions Trophy

The Men's Champions Trophy is an annual event featuring the world's top-ranked teams, competing in a round-robin format in which each team plays all other teams. Six teams qualify to play for the trophy.

## Women's international hockey

The International Federation of Women's Hockey Associations (IFWHA) was formed in 1927, and became part of the International Hockey Federation (FIH) in 1982. The FIH organizes the Women's World Cup and the Women's Champions Trophy.

### Women's World Cup

The Women's World Cup began in 1974 and is now held every four years. Teams in different parts of the world play a series of qualifying games to advance to the finals of the World Cup. Past World Cup winners were:

- Netherlands, 1974
- West Germany, 1976
- Netherlands, 1978
- West Germany, 1981
- Netherlands, 1983
- Netherlands, 1986
- Netherlands, 1990
- Australia, 1994
- Australia, 1998
- Argentina, 2002.

**The team from Argentina and their coaches celebrate winning the 2002 Women's World Cup for hockey held in Perth, Western Australia.**

### Women's Champions Trophy

The Women's Champions Trophy began in 1987 and is an annual event that features the world's top-ranked teams competing in a round-robin format in which each team plays all other teams. Six teams qualify to play for the trophy.

**Did you know?**

The 1998 World Cup in Utrecht, the Netherlands, was the first time that both men's and women's tournaments were held at the same time in the same host city.

# Olympic hockey

Hockey is called Field Hockey at the Olympics. The first Olympic hockey competition for men was held in London in 1908. The sport was dropped from the Stockholm Games in 1912 but was included for the 1920 Antwerp Games. It was dropped again in 1924 because the sport had no international federation.

Hockey has been a permanent Olympic sport for men since the Amsterdam Games in 1928 and for women since the Moscow Games in 1980.

### Did you know?

The first time an Australian women's hockey team competed in the Olympics was in 1984 at Los Angeles. The team finished in fourth place. The women's team won gold medals in Seoul (1988), Atlanta (1996), and Sydney (2000).

Australian Nikki Hudson (left) and South African Marsha Marescia (right) playing during the Athens 2004 Olympics

# Glossary

| | |
|---:|---|
| **attackers** | players who try to score when their team is in possession of the ball |
| **crossbar** | the horizontal bar at the top of the goal |
| **defenders** | players positioned near the goalkeeper who try to prevent the other team from scoring |
| **dribble** | to run with the ball while keeping the stick close to the ball |
| **flick** | a push pass in which the ball is raised into the air with a quick movement of the stick; the ball must not rise more than 18 inches above the playing surface |
| **fouls** | when a player performs an action that breaks the rules |
| **jab** | to poke at the ball in an attempt to make the attacking player lose possession |
| **kevlar** | an artificial material that is extremely strong |
| **midfielders** | players positioned in the middle of the field who attack and defend |
| **pass** | to raise the stick and follow through in order to hit the ball to another player |
| **pass-back** | when a player at center field passes the ball back to a member of their team; used to start the game, at the start of the second half, or to restart play after a goal has been scored |
| **penalty** | when a player breaks a rule and the other team is given an advantage |
| **pitch** | a rectangular area on a field on which hockey is played |
| **push** | to push the ball with the stick while keeping both the ball and the head of the stick in contact with the ground |
| **reverse stick** | when the stick is turned so that the blade or flat side of the stick points to the right, allowing a hit or push in that direction |
| **scans** | watches for opponents while in possession of the ball |
| **tackle** | an attempt to take the ball away from the opponent, using the stick |

# Index

## A
aerial trap 15
attacking 9

## B
backhand receiving 15
block tackle 20

## C
cards 24
Champions Trophy 28–29
chip shot 19
clothing 7
competitions 28–30

## D
defending 9
dive shot 18
dodging 13
dribbling 5, 12–13

## E
edge shot 19

## F
field goals 23
fitness 26–27
flick 17
forehand push pass 16
forehand receiving 14

## G
goal circle 8
goalkeeping 5, 7, 21
goals 5, 8, 18–19, 23
grip 10

## H
history of hockey 4, 28–30
hitting 17, 18
hockey ball 6
hockey stick 5, 6

## I
Indian dribble 13
International Federation of Women's Hockey Associations (IFWHA) 29
International Hockey Federation (FIH) 4, 22, 28

## J
jab tackle 20

## M
midfielders 9

## O
Olympic hockey 30

## P
pass-back 5, 9
passing 16–17
penalty corner 23
penalty stroke 23
pitch 5, 8
player positions 9, 23
protective gear 7
push pass 16–17

## Q
quick hit 18

## R
receiving 14–15
reverse receiving 15
reverse tackle 20
rules 7, 8, 12, 19, 20, 21, 22, 24
running 11

## S
scoring 5, 18–19, 23
shooting 18–19
slide shot 18
stance 9
stretching 26–27

## T
tackling 10, 20
timing 5, 23
turning the stick 10

## U
umpires 5, 24–25
umpires' signals 25

## W
warming up 26–27
World Cup 28–29